Randy Riley's Really Big Hit

CHRIS VAN DUSEN

CANDLEWICK PRESS

Randy Riley stood at bat.
　　He gazed out at the mound.
His knees began to tremble,
　　and his heart began to pound.

Then Randy started thinking
　　about the pitcher's throw.
He wondered, without gravity,
　　how far the ball would go.

And as he stood there pondering,
　　strike three went whizzing by.
"YOU'RE OUT!" he heard the umpire call,
　　then walked off with a sigh.

See, Randy was a genius;
　　he just couldn't hit the ball.
He struck out every time at bat.
　　He wasn't good at all.
But something beyond baseball
　　brought a smile to Randy's face.
What Randy Riley really loved
　　was stuff from outer space!

He studied all the planets.
  He memorized their tilt.
He researched how the thrusters
  on the rocket ships were built.
He knew the constellations
  and the light-years to the stars.
And wouldn't it be great, he thought,
  to ride a bike on Mars?

When Randy Riley got back home,
he went up to his room.
He knew he stunk at baseball,
and it filled his heart with gloom.

So he took his favorite robots
from the shelf above his bed
and staged a game of baseball
with his robot team instead.

That night before he went to sleep,
    Randy scanned the sky,
and through his Space Boy telescope
    a glimmer caught his eye.

He fiddled with the focus
    till he saw it crystal clear;
it was a massive fireball,
    and it was coming near!

Alarmed, he started plotting
    the projection of its path.
He formulated diagrams.
    He double-checked his math.

He calculated quickly
    and concluded, with a frown:
in nineteen days, the fireball
    would crash into his town!

Randy Riley flew downstairs
to warn his mom and dad.
The impact would be major,
and the damage would be bad!

He explained the situation
until his face was red,
but they told him he was tired,
and they sent him off to bed.

$x(d) = -0.002d^2 + 0.17d + 5$

$h \cong 91$ ft.

3.17

Poor Randy couldn't sleep at all;
he thought the whole night through.
By morning it was obvious
just what he had to do.

He gathered what he needed
with determined resolution
and lugged it off behind the shed
to work on his solution.

Randy toiled for eighteen days
while other kids had fun.
But he was on a mission,
so he worked till he was done.

At breakfast on the nineteenth day,
the news announcer said,
"This is a special bulletin!
Emergency! Code red!

A fireball's approaching!
It just flew past the moon!
It's coming fast, so be prepared
for it to hit by noon!"

Everybody burst outside
as fear and panic grew!
But Randy ran back to the shed—
he had a job to do.

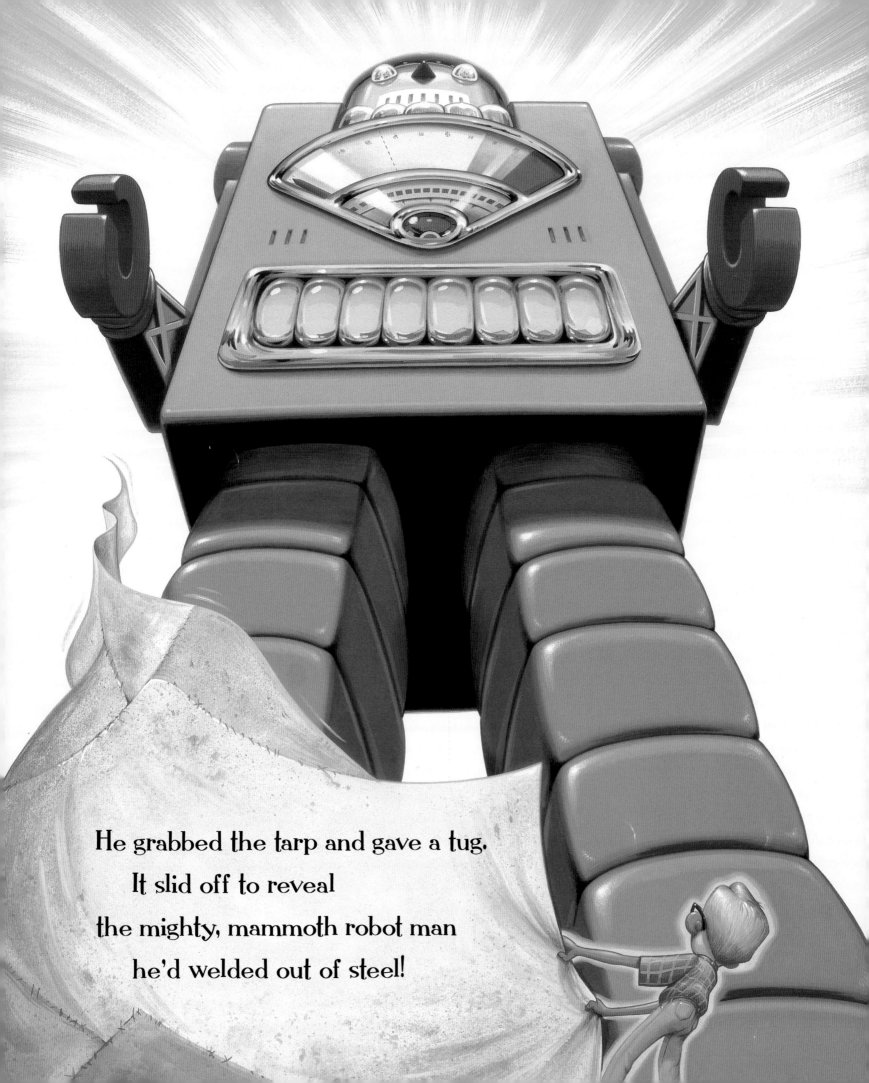

He grabbed the tarp and gave a tug.
It slid off to reveal
the mighty, mammoth robot man
he'd welded out of steel!

The robot needed power,
  and Randy knew precisely
that ninety-seven batteries
  would energize it nicely.

The eyes lit up. The engine whirred.
  Step one was now complete.
So far, so good, thought Randy.
  Then they thundered down the street.

Step two of Randy's mission
    took place just south of town,
in a section known as Millville,
    where he slowed the robot down.

The robot ripped the smokestack
    off an old, abandoned mill,
then Randy turned the throttle knob
    to march him up the hill.

Back in town, the people
were as frightened as could be,
but Randy knew the time had come
for critical step three.

The robot burst out through the trees,
stepped up, and took a stance,
while everyone fell silent,
as if frozen in a trance.

Randy's eye was on the ball.

No room for error now.

Three-two-one and FLIP THE SWITCH!

A *SWOOSH* and then . . .

A blinding FLASH! A booming *CRASH!*
He knew what he had done;
Randy Riley had a HIT!
His VERY FIRST HOME RUN!

The fireball sailed out of sight.
A rousing cheer began:
"Hooray for Randy Riley
and his giant metal man!"

And as the crowd went crazy,
Randy stood there with a grin
and mumbled, "How predictable—
a fastball, low and in."

When things returned to normal
after Randy saved the day,
he went back to the baseball field
to join his friends at play.

And though he swings in earnest,
he rarely hits the ball.
But that's OK 'cause Randy's had
the BIGGEST HIT OF ALL!

To Eliot Charles Zeiner Piper, Genius

Special thanks to my title consultants, the Riley family

Copyright © 2012 by Chris Van Dusen

First edition 2012

Library of Congress Cataloging-in-Publication Data

Van Dusen, Chris.
Randy Riley's really big hit / Chris Van Dusen. — 1st ed.
p. cm.
Summary: Randy Riley, a science genius who loves baseball but is not very good at it,
needs to use both his interests to save his town from a giant fireball that is heading their way.
ISBN 978-0-7636-4946-3
[1. Stories in rhyme. 2. Baseball —Fiction. 3. Robots —Fiction.] I. Title.
PZ8.3.V335Ran 2012
[E] —dc23   2011018609

15 16 APS 10 9 8 7 6

Printed in Humen, Dongguan, China

This book was typeset in Malonia Voigo.
The illustrations were done in gouache.

Candlewick Press
99 Dover Street
Somerville, Massachusetts 02144

visit us at www.candlewick.com